This book belongs to

_____

_____

Aged _____

STORIES FOR THE YOUNG READER

THE
Teddy Bear's Picnic

AND OTHER STORIES

STORIES FOR THE YOUNG READER

THE
Teddy Bear's Picnic

AND OTHER STORIES

p

This is a Parragon Book
This edition published in 2002

Parragon
Queen Street House
4 Queen Street
Bath BA1 1HE, UK

Copyright © Parragon 2000

ISBN 0-75258-421-9

Designed by Mik Martin

Printed in Italy

These stories have been previously
published by Parragon in the
Bumper Bedtime Series

CONTENTS

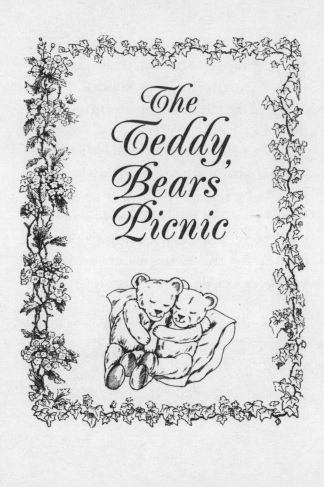

ONE DAY, Mrs Carolinus, who taught the smallest children at the nursery school, clapped her hands for attention and used her loudest voice.

"Children!" she called. "I have a special announcement to make, and you will each have a letter to take home to your parents. Next week we shall have a special outing to raise money for the new playground. It will be a Teddy Bears' Picnic! You

can each bring your bears — but only one teddy bear each, please — and something nice to eat or drink. I'm sure we shall all have a lovely day."

The children were very excited at the news.

"My teddy bear's name is Honey," said Lauren. "He'll love coming to a picnic."

"My teddy bear has beautiful white fur and a special stripey jacket all of his own," said Carla. "He's been all over the place. I took him with me when we went overseas on holiday last year, so a little picnic won't be so exciting for *him*."

"I don't know *which* of my

teddy bears to bring," said Annabelle grandly. "I've got *ten*, you know. Some of them are really too beautiful to bring outside, and others are *huge*, so I really couldn't carry them. I'll have to think about what to do."

One little girl listened to her friends talking and kept very quiet. Sally only had one teddy bear, but she loved him more than all her other toys. He was very old and rather threadbare. Two of his paws had worn out and been replaced by Sally's Mum, so he now had two blue paws and two pink paws. What Sally loved best about Rory (for that was her bear's name) was that he had been given to her by her Granny,

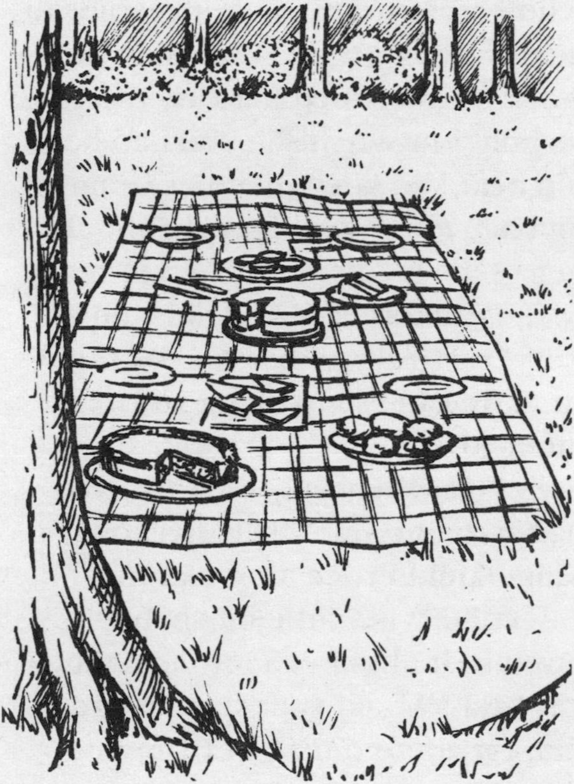

who had moved two years earlier to live far away on the other side of the world. Sally missed her Granny terribly, but when she cuddled her old bear, she knew that her Granny loved her and was thinking about her.

"The other girls will laugh at Rory," said Sally to herself. "Poor old bear. He can't help being worn and mended."

But when Sally took the letter home to her Mum that afternoon, Mum couldn't see a problem.

"Rory is a little bit shabby because he has been loved so much," she said. "Would you want to swap him for a brand new bear?"

"Oh no," said Sally. "Never!"

The day of the picnic soon arrived. The weather was bright and sunny — just right for a lovely day out of doors. Sally's Mum had made some chocolate buns and some cheese rolls for her to take to share with the other children. She wrapped them up and put them in Sally's school bag.

"There doesn't seem to be much room in here, Sally," said her mother as she tried to tuck the food away. "Just a minute. What's this? You've put Rory in the bottom of your bag! He won't be able to see anything in there! Poor old bear!"

Sally hung her head. "I'm sorry,"

she said. "I was just afraid that the others would laugh at him, because he's not fluffy and new, you know."

"The only important thing is what *you* think about your teddy bear," said Mum. "If you don't laugh at him, it doesn't matter one bit what other people think. What would Granny say if she could see Rory hidden away?"

Sally knew that her mother was right. She put her bag over one shoulder and tucked Rory under the other arm.

"Come along, Rory," she said. "We've got a picnic to go to!"

Mum took Sally and Rory to the place where everyone was

meeting for the picnic. It was on the outskirts of a beautiful wood. Mrs Carolinus had a list of all the children's names, and she ticked them off as they arrived.

Soon there were twenty children, all clutching their teddy bears, waiting to set off. Two other teachers had come along to help Mrs Carolinus.

"Now, before we go," called Mrs Carolinus, "I want you all to listen very carefully to what I have to say." (She was using her loudest voice again.) "It is very easy to get lost in a wood like this one," she went on, "so you must all keep up with the person in front. No dawdling! And no one, whatever happens, must stray off the path. Do you all understand?"

"Yes, we understand!" called the children.

"Then we are ready to begin," said Mrs Carolinus. "Quick march, everyone!"

The teachers and the children set off. To begin with they walked side by side, but soon the path through the trees became narrower,

so they had to walk in single file. In places, bushes and brambles almost covered the path, so the teachers had to hold them out of the way as the children went past. Mrs Carolinus called out all the time to make sure that no one got lost.

"Are you there, Annabelle? All right, Sally? Keep up, Carla!"

The children had to concentrate so hard on following the person in front that there was no time to look at other bears or compare them. Sally began to feel better.

"This *is* an adventure, isn't it, Rory?" she whispered.

When they had been walking

for about half an hour, and were deep in the forest, Mrs Carolinus called out very loudly.

"Everybody stop!"

Unfortunately, some children stopped more quickly than others, so there was quite a bit of confusion and one or two dropped teddy bears. Soon everyone had picked themselves up and dusted themselves down. Mrs Carolinus called out again.

"Now we can't stop here for our picnic because there are too many bushes and brambles," she said. "We will have to walk a little way from the path to find a clearing where we can all sit down together."

"But I thought she said we mustn't leave the path?" whispered Carla.

She knows best," said Annabelle. "After all, she *is* a teacher."

One by one, the children and teachers followed Mrs Carolinus, until they found a lovely clearing where they could spread out a cloth and all the delicious things they had brought to eat.

What a feast it was! And Sally didn't have to worry about anyone thinking Rory was old and shabby because everyone was much too interested in having something to eat to notice *what* her bear looked like.

At last, the children and the teachers could not eat any more. In fact, there was not very much *left* to eat! Walking in the woods had certainly given everyone an appetite. Mrs Carolinus called out again.

"We shouldn't start walking again immediately after our picnic," she said. "We must give our tummies a chance to settle. Let's sing some songs instead. Now, who knows any songs about teddy bears?"

The children had a lovely time. They sang the song about teddy bears bouncing on the bed and the one about the three bears. And, of course, they sang the song about the teddy bears' picnic — twice!

"Now, collect up your things," said Mrs Carolinus, "and please be very careful not leave anything behind. We must leave these beautiful woods as free of litter as we found them. And whatever you do, *don't* leave your teddy bears behind!"

"As if I'd leave you, Rory," whispered Sally, as they all formed a line once more.

But for the first time, Mrs Carolinus seemed a little bit uncertain. She looked around and had a few words with the other teachers.

The children saw them shaking their heads and looking a little worried. Finally, Mrs Carolinus spoke up.

"It's this way!" she called. But her voice didn't sound quite as sure as it usually did.

The children and the teachers walked for five minutes before Mrs Carolinus told everyone to stop and not to move.

"We should have reached the path by now," she said, "so I think we are slightly off course. Follow me, and we'll soon be back on track."

The children followed their teacher, whispering excitedly to each other. "Do you think we're lost?" they asked. "What are we going to do if we can't find our way home?"

Five minutes later, Mrs Carolinus called a halt again.

"This way isn't quite right either," she said. "The other teachers and I are just going to have a little talk about the best way home. Don't wander off!"

The children sat down on a nearby grassy bank. Now, for the first time, they looked at each other's bears.

"Goodness me, Sally," said Annabelle, "what a very old bear you've got there. It must be nearly an antique!"

"Yes, he's very valuable," said Sally, which wasn't strictly true, but it made her feel better, and

Annabelle didn't say anything else about Rory.

After ten minutes, Carla, who had been keeping an eye on the little group of teachers, leaned forward and whispered to the others. "You know," she said, "I think we really *are* lost. I just heard Mrs Carolinus say that the best thing would be to stay where we are and wait for someone to come to look for us."

"But it will get dark!" said Annabelle. "I don't want to be in this creepy wood when it's dark!"

"Well, I don't think anyone knows the way home," said Carla, "so we don't have much choice really."

Just then, Sally heard a little whispering sound in her ear. It was Rory, trying as hard as he could to attract her attention.

"What is it, Rory?" Sally asked her old bear.

"I couldn't help overhearing what you were saying," said Rory, "and I'd like to suggest that you give

the *bears* a chance to find the way home."

"Whatever do you mean?" asked Sally in surprise.

"Well," said Rory quietly, so that the other children couldn't hear, "I don't expect anyone has thought of this, but bears are used to woods and forests. That's the kind of place they come from, after all. We notice things that human beings never think about, such as whether a tree might have bark for a bear to scratch, or where there might be a hollow tree trunk to shelter in when it is cold and wet."

"So what?" hissed Sally.

"So I think I can tell the

difference between one tree and the next much better than that teacher of yours," explained Rory. "But you'll have to pretend it was you who noticed, because she'll never believe me."

Sally looked long and hard at her bear. "Why don't the other bears know the way as well?" she asked slowly.

"Perhaps some of them do," said Rory. "I haven't had a chance to ask them. But, you know, most of the bears here are rather *young*. They probably haven't learnt very much about woodcraft yet."

Sally was convinced. She and Rory whispered together for a few more minutes. Then the little girl picked up her bear and made her way to where Mrs Carolinus was sitting, looking rather anxious and upset.

"Excuse me," said Sally, politely, "but I think we are really very near the path, you know. I'm quite sure we passed that tree with the silvery bark on our way here."

Mrs Carolinus looked very doubtful, but she was ready to clutch at any straw. She sent one of the other teachers over to the silvery tree to have a look. Two minutes later, the teacher was waving excitedly. It *was* the path! They were not lost after all!

It was a tired but happy group of teachers and children who found their way to the meeting place half an hour later. The parents had begun to look at their watches, wondering what had happened to the party.

"Ah," said Mrs Carolinus quickly, "there were so many good opportunities for nature study in the woods, I'm afraid we rather lost track of time."

"We certainly lost track of something," whispered Rory, with a giggle.

That night, when Mum tucked Sally up in her bed, she asked what the other children had thought of Rory.

"They said he was old and shabby," said Sally, "but you know, I don't mind at all. There's a lot to be said for being old."

Mum couldn't help but smile at Sally's serious little face. "I'll tell Granny you said that!" she laughed, turning out the light.

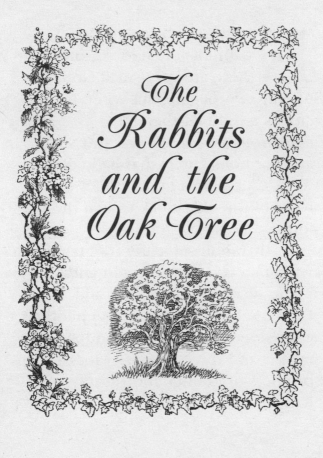

The
Rabbits
and the
Oak Tree

Now THERE ARE large families, with lots of children, and there are very small families of only two people, but when it comes to rabbits, there are *enormous* families. It was just such an enormous family that had taken up residence in a home under the roots of the oldest oak tree in the forest.

By rabbit standards, the family wasn't so very big to begin with. There were Mother Rabbit and Father Rabbit with their six children. There were two sets of grandparent rabbits and three or four sisters and brothers of Mother and Father Rabbit — *and* their children.

Altogether, there must have been about thirty lively little rabbits.

The oak tree had lived in the forest for hundreds of years. Its roots were thick and twisted. As soon as he saw them, Father Rabbit knew that he could dig a very fine home among those roots, and that is exactly what he did. And the oak tree didn't seem to mind.

But over the next few years, the rabbit family didn't so much grow as *explode*! The children had children, and the children's children had children. Very soon there were over two hundred rabbits living under the oldest oak tree in the forest.

Of course, some expansion had been necessary. You can't squeeze more and more rabbits into a small space (unless you are a conjuror). So Father Rabbit and his brothers and cousins and nephews dug more and more passages and rooms among the roots of the tree. I must say they did it beautifully. There were cosy little bedrooms and spacious sitting rooms. There were places for the baby rabbits to play and quiet spots where the older rabbits could sit and chat and have a little peace.

But as the months passed, the oak tree began to feel worried. It seemed that his roots were not planted so firmly in the soil as they once had been. Where once he had enjoyed feeling the breeze whistling through his leaves, now he felt uneasy and just a little bit wavering and wobbly. Winter was coming, and the oak tree dreaded the gales that sometimes rushed through the wood.

"I don't know what to do," he muttered to the much younger birch tree standing near him.

The birch tree was very flattered. It was usually she who asked the ancient oak tree for advice. She rustled her branches and thought as hard as possible.

"I'm sure those rabbits don't mean to do you harm," she said. "The trouble is that it's not easy for a tree to talk to a rabbit. They just don't speak the same kind of language. What you need is an interpreter. Someone who can understand both sides."

"By Jove, you're right!" cried the oak tree. "And there is only one woodland creature who can do such a thing. We need to find a woodsprite."

You have probably never seen a woodsprite, for they are so small and flit about so quickly that the best you can usually do is to *think* you've caught sight of one out of the corner of your eye. If you have ever noticed a leaf waving more vigorously than its neighbours, or seen the sunshine sparkling on a drop of water as it shimmers on a cobweb, you have probably almost seen a woodsprite. They are very difficult to find.

Luckily, ancient trees know a little of the old magic. The oak tree gave a kind of a rumble and little bit of a creak. It almost sounded as if it was singing. In fact, it was calling to the woodsprites to come to its aid.

In only a few moments, a little creature flitted across the clearing to the oak tree. It could have been a dried leaf, drifting in the breeze. It could have been a butterfly, alighting on a branch. It could have been a clump of fluffy dandelion seeds, floating through the air. But it wasn't. It was a woodsprite, answering the call of the mighty oak tree.

It did not take the tree long to explain the problem.

The woodsprite nodded her head and flitted down one of the holes at the base of the tree. She travelled through tunnel after tunnel, until, as luck would have it, she came face to face with Father Rabbit, who was munching his dinner.

"Hello," said the rabbit politely. "How can I help you?"

"I'm very much afraid that you

are damaging the mighty oak above you," said the woodsprite, in a voice that was no louder than a feather falling on to a bed of moss.

"Damaging it? How?" asked the rabbit in surprise. "I thought he quite liked us living here. We feel so safe among his strong roots."

"That's just the problem," explained the woodsprite. "Your burrows have loosened the roots so much that the oak tree fears the next strong wind could cause him to fall.

"Well," said the rabbit slowly, "I don't mean to sound uncaring, but all trees must fall sometime, and the oak tree has reached a very great age."

"And could reach an even greater one," said the woodsprite. "And what do you think will happen if the tree *does* fall? Its roots will come tearing out of the ground, destroying your home and leaving your burrows open, so that any passing fox or owl could carry off your little ones."

"When you put it like that," said the rabbit, "I can see that it is our duty to help the noble tree. But it seems to me that the only way we can help is to move altogether, and leave our beautiful home."

"No, no," said the sprite. "Not ten minutes from here is a lovely patch of heath, with sandy soil and thorny bushes above. It is the perfect spot for you to dig a new home, and you will be much safer there. And if you fill in most of the burrows in this home, you could keep a smaller, holiday home here to visit in turns whenever you need a break."

That sounded an excellent idea, so the rabbit hopped off to

call a family meeting to discuss the matter.

A couple of hours later, the oak tree felt a squiggly, wriggly feeling around his roots, as the rabbits started to fill in a large number of their burrows and bedrooms. Before nightfall, the tree felt much happier than he had done for weeks. His roots gripped the soil firmly, and he could allow his branches to wave without feeling that he was about to topple over. He gave a happy sigh and settled down to grow for another five hundred years or so.

Meanwhile, the rabbits were having a wonderful time in the sandy heath. In fact, they enjoyed it so much that they very soon had no wish at all to visit their holiday home under the oak tree.

So do the burrows stand empty, filling up gradually with dried leaves? No, someone has moved in who flits so lightly along the passageways that the oak tree feels his toes are being tickled. Next time you hear an oak tree giggle, don't be surprised. It is simply that a woodsprite is not far away.

The First Christmas Tree

O N A VERY SPECIAL NIGHT, long, long ago, a star shone down upon a stable. Night after night, it shone, until some wise men, travelling from the East, reached the building over which it hovered. They went inside to offer gifts of gold, frankincense and myrrh to the baby they found inside.

Later, the baby and its parents were warned of danger, and they packed their belongings in the night and journeyed on to Egypt. Few people know that the star also continued on its travels, wandering across the dark sky in search of a final resting place.

The star travelled over the

desert, and looked down on mile
upon mile of barren sand. As the
winds blew, the sand was constantly
shifted from place to place, forming
mountains and valleys that were
never still. That was no place for a
star to rest.

As the star journeyed, it
crossed the ocean. Far below, the
restless waves were in ceaseless
motion. Over and over again, they

rose and fell, for the ocean is never at peace. The star could not find a final stopping place on the restless seas.

The star travelled on, and many people looked up into the night sky and pointed at the shining visitor.

"What does it mean? Will it bring us good luck or bad?" they asked each other.

But the star carried no luck. It simply shone by night and became dark by day, always travelling to find a place to stay.

The star travelled over the mountains, as cold and bright in the moonlight as the star itself. On their peaks, the snow lay unchanging, but

on the slopes below, it sometimes
drifted into heaps and sometimes
melted into a fast-flowing river,
gushing down the rocky mountain
face to the valleys beneath. Even the
unchanging mountains endlessly
shifted and shrugged, sometimes
sending down huge shelves of snow
as avalanches. The star could not rest
on a mountain top.

On its journey, the star
travelled over towns and cities,
where lights burned as brightly by
night as they did by day. In the
orange glow given off by a thousand
lamps and candles, the star could
hardly be seen. It could not come to
rest in such a place as that.

When it came to the great empty wastes of the Arctic, the star believed that it had found a home as pure and changeless as itself. It hovered above the North Pole and saw itself reflected far below in the great sheets of ice that cover the sea. Everything was cold, cold and silent. The star looked down on the earth and felt disconnected and alone. It found that what it sought was peace, not emptiness.

Moving south again, the star came to a great forest. In the moonlight, its trees seemed clothed in dark green robes. Here and there, frost sugared their branches, and tiny creatures huddled to keep warm.

The trees were majestic, straight and tall, and they were growing. With every second that passed, the trees were reaching higher and higher, slowly stretching nearer and nearer to the star. For a long time, the star hovered over the forest, not knowing where to come to rest.

Then, far below, it saw that the trees were beginning to thin. Further south, they did not stand in serried ranks but grew singly, tall and proud. One tree in particular seemed to stand as a bridge between the earth and sky, its roots firmly in the soil, while its topmost branches brushed the stars.

The special star floated gently

above the mighty tree, so that its pure, white light lay cleanly upon the feathery branches. This was the place where it would stay, in touch with all above and below.

At Christmas time, when we remember the baby in the stable and the star that shone, night after night, above the poor building, many people bring a fir tree into their homes and place a silver star at its very top. It is a reminder that the star of the first Christmas, although it was far too high and heavenly to be reached by people on earth, still shed light into their lives, and came to rest with all the living things here below.

The Song of Spring

THERE WAS ONCE a little bird who lived in a tree on the edge of a wood. All year long, she was as busy as could be. In spring, she chose a site for her new nest and gathered twigs and moss to build it. Then she laid her eggs and settled down to hatch them.

She only left the eggs for seconds at a time, when she hopped off to find a quick snack. It was during one of these very short breaks that something strange happened in the little bird's nest. When she returned, one of her eggs seemed to have grown bigger!

"That's odd," said the little bird to herself. "It has never happened before." But the egg was the right shape and the right colour. The little bird wondered if she had become so tired sitting on the eggs that she could no longer think properly. She decided to have a quick snooze and settled down comfortably once again.

Day after day, the little bird sat on her nest, keeping the eggs snug and warm.

"Soon I shall hear that first

little *tap tap*," she said to herself. "Then I shall see my darling little children. I can hardly wait."

Sure enough, the little bird woke one morning to a tiny sound under her feathers. *Tap tap! Tap tap!*

Soon a little crack appeared in one of the eggs, and a tiny orange

beak poked through. It was followed by a sleepy little head and a damp little body. Then the new nestling sat quietly in the sun until his feathers dried.

The little bird hardly had time to feel proud of her son before another *tap tap!* came from one of the other eggs. Once again, a little beak was followed by a little bird. Now there were two.

The little bird had to wait until evening for her third egg to hatch. This baby was just as beautiful as the first two.

The mother bird looked at the last egg. It was the largest of all. She listened hard, but could hear no tapping. Surely this egg was not going to be much longer?

One day passed and then another. The little bird did not know what to do. She needed to fly off to find food for her three little nestlings, but she did not like to leave the unhatched egg. At last, there was a very loud *TAP TAP!* and the last egg cracked in two. Out hopped a very strange bird indeed.

The mother bird felt a thrill of fear. She knew exactly what this bird was. It was a *cuckoo*. If she was not careful, it would push her other babies out of the nest.

The baby cuckoo stared at its

mother and opened its beak. It already wanted food.

"All right," said the bird, "I will feed you, but you must promise me not to harm any of my other babies. If you do, I will push *you* right out of the nest. Do you understand me?"

"*Quark*!" The young cuckoo understood very well.

That spring, the mother bird exhausted herself finding food for her brood. At last the day came when they flew away from the nest.

It was sad for the mother, but her heart swelled with pride when she heard a bird singing far away.

"*Cuckoo cuckoo!*"

"That's my boy," she said.

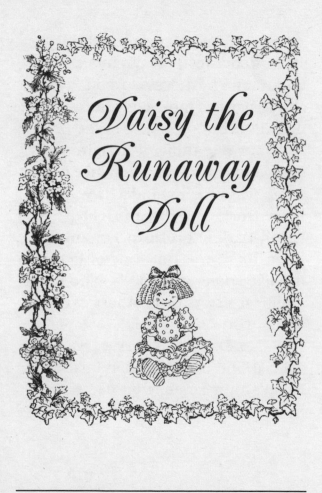

Daisy the Runaway Doll

DAISY FANCIED HERSELF the smartest, the most beautiful, the best dressed, and altogether the most elegant of all the dolls in Laura's room.

For one thing, although everyone called her Daisy, her full name was much grander. It was Daisy Dorinda Deborah Delilah Dinah Darlington Dean. For another thing, there was only one of her — not like some other dolls, who have identical sisters or brothers everywhere you care to look!

No, Daisy was very, very special. She had been handmade by Laura's Aunt Susan, who had given her to Laura for her fourth birthday.

Her eyes were made of shiny black
buttons. Her hair was made of the
finest sunflower-gold wool. Her
smile was sewn on with rosy red
thread. She had three beautiful
dresses, all with matching shoes and
lacy socks. She had her own suitcase
for all her finery and her own little
blue umbrella. She sat proudly in her
own special place on Laura's bed.

Laura took good care of Daisy.
Every day she combed her golden
hair, dressed her up in one of her
beautiful dresses, and took her out in
her buggy. Laura took Daisy to the
park, to the shops, and to visit
friends. Sometimes Laura had tea
parties, and Daisy was always the

guest of honour. Laura loved Daisy, and Daisy loved Laura, and they were happy together.

Things went on in this pleasant, carefree way for a long time. Then, one summer afternoon, something terrible happened.

A *dog* came to live with Laura and her parents. He was a big, sloppy, floppy-eared, tail-wagging, hairy, muddy-pawed spaniel called Max. And Laura loved *him*, just as she loved Daisy.

It wouldn't have been so bad if Max had stayed out in the garden. But to Daisy's dismay, he was allowed in the house with Laura and her mother and father. Max was even

allowed in Laura's room! And, to
Daisy's horror, he was sometimes
even allowed to jump up on the
bed! Then he would snuffle and
nuzzle Daisy with his big wet nose,
until Laura called him away.

"Come on, Max," Laura would say happily. "Catch the ball!" And she would grab her blue rubber ball and throw it into the air. Max, his ears flying and his tail flapping wildly, would leap into the air and catch the ball in his big, wet mouth. Then he would bound across the room, set the ball at Laura's feet, and wait for her to do it all again.

Max never watched where he was going, and he didn't care who or what was in the way. He often stepped on Laura's cuddly toys with his big clumsy paws. He knocked down her trucks and cars and books with his wagging tail. He crashed into the house where the little tiny dolls lived and knocked it over. And sometimes he picked up Laura's teddy bear and flung him right into the air!

The amazing thing was that neither Laura nor any of the other toys seemed to mind all this madness and mayhem. In fact, they all seemed to *enjoy* playing with Max! But Daisy didn't want any part of his rowdy games, and she always shrank back when she heard Max's bark.

But the more she shrank back, the more Max seemed to want to play with her. "Come on!" he would yap at Daisy. "Please play with me! I'll give you a ride in the air! Old Teddy loves it, and you might too!"

"Go away, you monster!" Daisy would hiss at Max when Laura's back was turned. "Leave me alone! Just leave me alone!"

One morning towards the end of summer, Laura got dressed in some smart new clothes.

"I'm starting school today," she

told Daisy, "so I won't be able to play with you so much. But don't worry. Max will look after you, won't you, Max?"

Right behind her, Max wagged his tail enthusiastically.

Later, when Daisy heard the door close behind Laura and her Mum, she dreaded what would happen next. Any minute now…

"*Woof! Woof!* Who's ready for some fun?" barked Max, as he came hurtling into the room with his floppy ears flying.

"I am! I am!" shouted Old Teddy. "I want to go flying high in the air!"

"We are! We are!" squealed the

little tiny dolls. "Let's play 'Earthquake' again, Max, where you rattle the dolls' house and make everything wobbly!"

"I'm ready, Max!" called Cuddly Bunny. "Play 'Elephant Steps' on my tummy, Max!"

But Max knew who *he* wanted to play with. He leapt up on to the bed and bounded towards Daisy, the dainty doll.

"Come on, Daisy," he barked, tugging at her arm. "You'll have fun, really!"

"Leave me alone!" snapped Daisy. "Go away, before you mess up my golden hair and tear my beautiful clothes!"

"I'll be careful," barked Max eagerly. "I promise!"

"No," said Daisy, "no, no, NO!"

So Max went off to play with the other toys until Laura came home again.

The same thing happened the next day, and the next. Each morning, Max would jump up on the bed and say, "Please will you play with me today, Daisy?" And each day, Daisy's answer was exactly the same.

"No, no, no. And that is *final*!"

But Max just would not give up, and after several weeks of this, one morning he went too far. He tugged and tugged at Daisy's arm until he pulled the sleeve of her beautiful dress right off!

"Now look what you've done!" shouted Daisy. "That does it. I'm leaving. I have to go away and find another home — one without a *dog*!"

And with that, Daisy climbed down from the bed, packed all her things in her carrying case, and ran out of the room. A moment later, she was *thumpety-thumpety-thumpeting* down the stairs, trailing her case and her own special blue umbrella behind her.

"Daisy, wait!" called Max. "What will Laura say?"

"Come back, Daisy! Come

back!" cried Old Teddy, Cuddly Bunny and the little tiny dolls.

But Daisy was not turning back. She ran into the living room, clambered up on to the sofa, and went right out through the open window. A second later, she was in the flowerbed in the front garden.

It had rained the night before, and the flowerbed was muddy and damp. As Daisy stood up, she realised that her blue dress was a bit stained and soggy.

"Never mind," she thought. "I have to keep going. I'll be all right once I've found a lovely new home."

Daisy had never been out on her own before, but she had been out with Laura dozens and dozens of times. She knew the way to Laura's friend Katie's house. She knew the way to the shops. And she knew the way to the park.

So Daisy picked up her case and her umbrella and began making her way down the garden. *Squelch, squelch, squelch, splotch* went her smart shoes in the mud. Her lacy white socks were soon soaked through, and she began to feel cold, but she made herself keep going.

By the time Daisy reached the pavement, it was nearly midday. She was exhausted. It is one thing to be pushed somewhere in a buggy, but quite another to have to walk there

on your own little legs. No wonder
the poor doll was tired! But Daisy
knew she had a long way to go, and
she wanted to get to the park before
nightfall, so she didn't stop.

As Daisy started her journey
down the pavement, the wind
began to blow and the sky grew
grey. Moments later, big heavy
raindrops plopped down on to
Daisy. She struggled to put up her
little blue umbrella, but it was so
tiny that the big drops of rain
simply splashed over the edge and
into her face. Soon her clothes and
her hair were soaked. In fact,
Daisy's whole self, right through to
her insides, was drenched and cold.

She was shivering terribly and felt faint.

"It's no use," Daisy said to herself. "I'll have to stop and rest, just for a bit. There are some leaves under those big trees … they'll be soft to lie on … I'll just rest for a little while … just a little while…" Wearily, Daisy collapsed on to the small pile of leaves. Her button eyes closed, and she fell fast asleep. All the while, the rain kept falling, and the wind kept blowing, colder and colder.

Hours later, Daisy woke with a start. The rain had stopped, but darkness surrounded the dainty doll. When she tried to move, she found

she couldn't. She was trapped in a
great heap of cold, wet leaves. In the
tree above her, an owl hooted eerily
and flapped its wings. The sound
made the poor doll even more
frightened. She was alone in a
strange place, with no one to help
her.

"Oh, what will happen to me
now?" Daisy thought, trembling with
cold and fear. Remembering Laura's
soft, warm bed — and Laura's soft,
warm arms around her — she began
to cry.

"Why did I ever run away?" she
sobbed. "How I wish I were back
home, safe with Laura!"

As she lay there in the leaves,

weeping and wishing, Daisy sudden-
ly heard something — a sound she
knew well. It was a bark, an excited,
happy bark, and it sounded so sweet
to Daisy.

"Max!" cried Daisy. "Max!
Help!" But she needn't have
bothered calling. Max knew just
where she was, and he was galloping

towards her. A moment later, she heard the familiar snuffle and felt Max's cold, wet nose nudging its way through the leaves. Then, ever so gently, Max grabbed hold of Daisy with his mouth and pulled her out.

"Oh, Max, you found Daisy!" cried Laura, running towards them. "Look, Mum!" she called. "Here she is! Oh, I can't believe it! Max found Daisy!"

When Laura took her and held her tight, Daisy felt happier than she ever had before.

"Let's have a look," said Laura's Mum, crouching down. "Hmm … I think after a wash in some warm, soapy water and a little work with a needle and thread, Daisy should look as beautiful as ever."

"It doesn't matter what she *looks* like, Mum," said Laura. "The important thing is that she's back — and Max found her! You're a very clever dog, Max! You're a very clever dog indeed!"

As Laura reached down to give Max a pat on the head, Daisy looked down at him, too. Max was the only one who noticed that at that moment, Daisy's smile grew just a little wider, and one of her shiny button eyes winked. It was a wink that said, "I think you're clever too — friend!"

The Toy Train

IN THE NURSERY CLASS, there were lots of toys for children to play with. The little ones came every day for two hours in the morning and two hours in the afternoon. They did painting — and painted their faces as well as their pictures. They did modelling — and had to be stopped from eating half the clay. They did dancing — and sometimes kicked each other only half by mistake. They did singing — and sometimes you could recognise the tune!

In the afternoon, the children had a quiet time, when the teacher read them a story. They had a mug of juice or milk and some fruit, and

some of them had a little sleep after-
wards as well. Then it was time to
play with the toys. And this time
frightened some of the toys very
much indeed.

"It isn't that they mean to be
rough," said the ragdoll, one evening

after the children had gone home. "That little boy with the curly hair wanted to play doctors, and he decided to chop my leg off! It was lucky the teacher noticed in time!"

The other toys shuddered at this dreadful story.

"It was the same for me," said the rocking horse, shaking her silky mane. "If only the teacher hadn't read a story about zebras to those silly children, they would never have tried to paint purple stripes on me!"

"Just think yourself lucky you don't have wheels," grumbled the truck. "I can't remember the last time I had a full set of four wheels. If one of them is found, another is lost, and I know that one of them is under the toy cupboard, where it will *never* be found. And don't talk to me about my suspension! It's no fun driving on your axles, I can tell you. No fun at all."

"You're right there," agreed the tractor, "and it's no fun being driven into walls and doors and people's legs either. And when a child bursts into tears, it's never their fault, you notice. Everyone complains that there are sharp bits on the toys. They say we're dangerous and should be … I can hardly say it … thrown away. I wouldn't have sharp bits if I hadn't been bashed into a wall over and over again!"

Now it happened about this time that a kind aunty gave the nursery class a brand new train for the children to play with. It had a shiny red funnel and bright blue paintwork. Its wheels were black, and its carriages were yellow. It even still had its own cardboard box!

The train had overheard the toys' complaints. "That kind of thing won't happen to me," it said to itself. "When they see how shiny and new I am, the children will be really careful with me."

The next day, the train was taken down from its shelf and given to a little girl to play with. She pushed it along quite happily for a while, but then she decided it needed some goods in its carriages. She put some modelling clay in the first one. She poured some paint in the second one. In the third carriage, she put half a sandwich left over from her lunch (and she had to squidge it a bit to make it fit). Then she had a wonderful time making the train crash into the long-suffering tractor.

By the time the children had put their coats on to go home, the train did not look like a new toy any more. Its paint was scratched and its funnel was bent. At least one of the teachers cleaned out its carriages and pushed the funnel back into shape before she went home.

That night, the toys grumbled as usual, and this time the train knew exactly what they were talking about.

"I'm not going to stay here with this kind of treatment," it said. "I'm off!" And to the amazement of the other toys, the train whizzed along the shelf and zoomed out of the top of the window, which happened to be open just far enough.

Crash! The train landed with a bump on the grass below, but all its carriages were still connected, so it felt ready for an adventure. The moon and stars were shining, as it set off to find a new home.

All that night, the little train whizzed along. At first it was travelling along pavements, but soon it came into the real countryside, where there were only roads with grass beside them. The little train soon found that it was not safe to chuff along on the roads. The puffing vehicle was too small for cars and trucks to see. One van almost squashed it, and another threw water from a puddle all over it. After that, the little train whizzed into a gateway and set off across a field.

It is not easy for trains to travel through tall grass and flowers, but as the sun rose, the little train felt quite cheerful. At least it was not about to be bashed or stuffed with stale sandwiches! All it needed to do was to find a new place to live, where it would be treated with some respect.

As luck would have it, the little train soon puffed into the garden of a large house. It was quite astonished to see another train whizzing towards it, travelling on a track laid all the way round the garden. The other train did not seem to want to stop to talk but zoomed past, blowing its whistle. The little train at once hopped on to the tracks and set off after it.

How much easier it was to travel on tracks! The little train enjoyed itself as it chuffed along. It was just giving a little *toot! toot!* as it went round a bend, when a large hand reached down and picked it up.

"Whatever is this?" asked a deep voice. It was the man who owned the house. He was a model-train collector, amazed to see a strange train chuffing round his tracks. "One of my friends must have put it here as a surprise," he said to himself. "Hmmm, it's not in very good condition. I must do some work on this one."

The train could hardly believe its luck. It soon found itself in the collector's workshop, where its scratches were painted and its funnel was made properly straight again.

By the time the man had finished, the train looked as good as new

— better than new, in fact, because it had been given a special polish that made it glisten and gleam.

Proudly, the man placed the train in a special cabinet, with a light above it so that everyone one could see how beautiful it looked. He wrote a little label and put it beside the train.

"I've really fallen on my wheels here," thought the train. "There could be no better place for a toy train to live."

It was true that the train never had to worry about being scratched and bashed. The man had so many different trains that he did not often take the little train from its cabinet.

Day after day, the little train sat there, looking perfect. There was not a speck of dust on its carriages or a smudge on its paintwork. It looked wonderful — and it *felt* very unhappy.

Isn't that train ever satisfied? you will ask. Sometimes it takes all of us a long time to find out what we really need. As it sat on its special shelf, the little train began to understand what all toys learn in the end: toys are meant to be played with, and they are not happy without children to love them — yes, and bash them and scratch them and squidge sandwiches into them sometimes as well.

It was several months before the little train had a chance to escape. Then, one evening, the collector took it into the garden for a whiz around the tracks. At the bottom of the garden, behind some bushes, the little train whizzed right off those tracks and off into the countryside.

It would be too much to expect that the little train found its way back to the nursery where it began, but it did find the house of a little girl and boy who were just delighted to have a new toy to play with. I would like to be able to tell you that they looked after the little train and were careful with it, but that wouldn't be true. They bashed it, they scratched it and they squidged not only sandwiches but several doughnuts and half a chocolate sponge cake into its carriages as well. Yes, they really loved their beautiful train.

And the little train? It has the kind of smile on his face that only a very bashed, scratched and squidged train can have. And, you know, it is as happy as a train can be.

The Lonely Panda

PAMELA **P**ANDA belonged to a little boy called Jack. He played with her a lot when he was small, but now that he was a much bigger boy, he preferred his trucks and his little kitchen and his farm.

Toys expect that kind of thing. They know that children grow up and pass on to other kinds of amusements. It is a little bit sad, but very often the old toys are able to play together (when human beings are not looking, of course), so they have a happy life. Later, if they are lucky, they may be given to another little boy or girl, who will love and care for them just as well as the first one did.

Pamela Panda was a beautiful fluffy black and white bear. She had been given to Jack when he was a baby, and he loved to chew her black ears and lay his little head on her white tummy. Several times during those early years, Pamela had got dirty and messy, but she was a very *washable* bear, so when Jack's Mum had given her a twirl in the washing machine, she came out looking like new.

The unfortunate thing was that Pamela was such a favourite with Jack in the early days that the other toys didn't get much of a chance to play with the little boy.

"It's not fair," grumbled the

twin teddy bears. "He plays with that panda all the time, and she's no better than we are."

"She thinks she's superior to the rest of us," said the toy train. "You can tell by the way she points her nose in the air. I don't think she's very friendly."

In fact, Pamela Panda pointed her nose just the way it had been made back in China, and the toys knew that really, but they were upset that they were hardly ever chosen as playthings, so they pretended not to like her.

As time went on, the toys forgot that they really didn't know anything about Pamela. The stories

they had made up about her being cold and stand-offish were told over and over again, until everyone simply assumed that they were true. So none of the other toys talked to the panda at all.

Pamela was hurt by the other toys' attitude, but she didn't mind too much while Jack was her best friend. And perhaps she didn't try quite as hard as she might have done to be friendly, knowing that she always had Jack to play with.

"You see, we were right," the twin teddies would say. "She *is* unfriendly, just as we said. Well, if that's the way she wants it…"

Very gradually, Jack grew up.

Soon he was crawling around the room and pulling himself up on the furniture. He did still play with Pamela, but he didn't chew her ears or stroke her tummy any more. No, now he picked her up and whirled her round his head by the arm, before throwing her as far as he could across the room.

"Ouch!" Pamela Panda was glad of her soft fur to cushion her landing. She really preferred *not* to be thrown around like that, but it was better than not being played with at all.

Very soon, Jack took his first wobbly steps. Pamela watched with pride, convinced that she had

helped him to grow so big and
strong. She would have liked to have
shared her pride with the other
toys, but when she turned to them,
they shrugged their shoulders and
looked away.

As soon as Jack was toddling
about the room, he lost interest in
Pamela. Oh, sometimes he jumped
up and down on her, and for a little
while he still liked to have her in his
bed at night, but more and more
now she was simply left on the
shelf. Poor Pamela felt very lonely.
Perhaps now the other toys would
be more friendly.

But during the day, the dolls
and bears talked to each other,

chattering so hard that there was no room for an outsider to make herself heard.

At night, the other toys cuddled up together, and the twin teddy bears had their own little cushion, where they slept next to each other. Poor Pamela didn't know whether the days or the nights were worse. She felt sad *all* the time.

About this time, Jack started to be very interested in books. He would sit with his Mum, turning the thick cardboard pages and looking at all the colourful pictures.

"Look, darling," his Mum would say, pointing to a picture of a truck, "that's just like your truck. And there

are some red boots, just like yours.
What else can you see on this
page?"

Jack would point to a picture
of a teddy bear and a train and try to
say the words.

"And look here," his Mum
would say. "Here's a picture of a
panda. Do you think it's a friend of
Pamela's?"

But Jack was bored now and
slipped off her lap to play with his
farm animals.

Jack's Mum put the book down
on a table, and as soon as her back
was turned, Pamela slipped across
and took a look at it. Yes, there was a
picture of a panda, and it looked just

like her! It had black ears and a white tummy, and it looked so friendly and cuddly. Pamela gave a big sigh. Why couldn't she have a twin like the teddy bears? It would be so lovely to have a friend to play with, especially a friend who was just like her!

Then Pamela had an idea. She had to wait until no one was around. Then she climbed up on to Jack's little stool and stood up. If she stood on the very tips of her paws, she could just reach to jump on to the dressing table, where Jack's Mum had put a large mirror.

Pamela raised her eyes slowly to the glass. There was another panda, just a pretty as she was, and it was smiling right at her!

"Hello!" said Pamela.

"Hello!" said the other panda.

Soon Pamela found that she could have lovely chats with the new panda.

At the back of her mind, of course, she knew that she was talking to her own reflection, but

she wanted so much to have a friend of her own that most of the time she didn't think about that.

The other toys simply didn't understand what she was doing.

"Just look at her," said the toy train. "She's so vain and stuck up she only ever wants to talk to herself. She's too good for us — at least, that's what *she* thinks!"

Things might have gone on in this unhappy way if Jack's cousin Joshua had not come to stay. Joshua was a year or so older than Jack and he was a *terror*!

Only two hours after Joshua's arrival, the toys were trembling in their shoes. He had stamped on the toy train. He had pulled the arms off the parachuting doll. He had made a little hole in the toy duck to see what his stuffing was made of. But worse was to follow.

That afternoon, Jack and his cousin went outside looking for adventures. They took with them some of the toys from Jack's room as part of the expedition team.

"We might want some of them to go first into dangerous places, to make sure it is safe," said Joshua wisely.

The toys shuddered as they were pulled along in the trolley that usually held Jack's bricks.

"What do you think they are

going to do with us?" whispered the twin teddy bears.

"Sshhh!" said the toy duck. "I've suffered enough already. I want them to forget I'm here."

Soon the boys reached the ditch at the end of the garden.

"We're not allowed to go across," said Jack. "Mum won't let me."

"No, but we could throw these toys across," said Joshua, "and see which ones can reach the other side."

Jack wasn't sure at first, but he was quite keen to show off his throwing, which, as we know, was pretty good.

"All right," he said. "I'll go first!"
And he picked up one of the twin
teddy bears and threw it as far as he
could, right over to the other side of
the ditch.

The boys had a lovely time,
before long both the bears, and the
toy duck, and Pamela Panda were
lying in a heap on the other side of
the ditch. Then Jack and Joshua
went off to have their lunch and
forgot all about the rest of their
expedition.

Out in the cold field, the toys
were moaning and groaning.

"We'll never be found here on
the ploughed earth. It's just the same
colour as our fur," said one of the

teddy bears. "We'll have to stay here all summer. Then the farmer will plough us up and that will be the end of us!"

But Pamela Panda was busy wriggling and jiggling on the bottom of the pile.

"Just let me get to the top," she puffed.

"Oh, that's typical," said the toy duck. "Why should you be on top of the pile, that's what I'd like to know?"

"Because," said Pamela, "I'm black and white. I'm the one that Jack's Mum will be able to see from far away when she comes to look for us this afternoon."

The toys were silent for a moment. What Pamela had said was certainly very sensible. They let her wriggle her way to the very top.

"Now," said Pamela, "it may be a long time before we are rescued, so I suggest we sing some songs and tell jokes. It will keep our spirits up."

The toys could hardly believe their ears. Was this the stuck-up panda who preferred her own company to theirs?

That afternoon, as they all lay together in the field, the toys learnt a lot more about Pamela, and she learnt a lot more about *them.* But one of the teddy bears was still not sure.

"What I don't understand," he said, "is why you spend so much time looking in the mirror. You're a fine looking panda, I know, but even so, it looks rather vain."

Then Pamela explained that she had been so lonely, she had talked to her own reflection sometimes, pretending it was another panda.

The toys were silent for a moment. Then they all spoke at once and from their hearts.

"We're sorry," they said. "Let's all be friends now, shall we?"

"Oh yes," agreed Pamela. "And here comes Jack's Mum. We'll soon be safe and sound."

The Singing Bear

ONCE UPON A TIME, there was a teddy bear with a beautiful voice. When you shook him gently, he made a deep, growling sound. When you poked his tummy, he made a friendly, humming sound. And when you patted him firmly on the back, he said quite distinctly, "Hello! I'm Bernard Bear!"

As you can imagine, Bernard Bear was a great favourite in the nursery. All the children loved to play with him, and best of all they liked to make him talk. In fact, if you shook, poked and patted Bernard in the right way, you could have quite a long conversation with him. It was lovely for the little ones.

But Bernard Bear was not content with the sounds he could make. He thought that he could do better. One day, a little girl brought a musical box to the nursery. When you opened the lid, a little dancer

inside twirled round and round, and music played. It was quite soft and tinkling, but everyone could hear that the musical box played "Twinkle, twinkle, little star."

Bernard Bear was most impressed by the box. "If a silly thing like that can sing a tune, then surely a clever bear like me can do it," he said to himself. "It's time I started to practise."

Bernard Bear was determined to sing at all costs. He took a deep breath and opened his mouth. "Grrrrr," he said. "Grrrrr. Grrrrr. Grrrrr."

Bernard Bear tried again. This time he took an even deeper breath.

"Hmmmm," he said. "Hmmmm. Hmmmm. Hmmmm."

This was no good at all. Bernard Bear took an enormous breath, so that he was full of air. He opened his mouth as wide as it would go. He clenched his paws and… "Hello!" he said. "I'm Bernard Bear!"

Poor Bernard! It didn't matter what he did or how hard he tried, he could only make the noises he had always been able to make. Of course, he could talk to other toys, but that wasn't what he wanted. He wanted to be able to sing to the children who played with him.

"You should think yourself

lucky," said the toy train. "I can only whistle to humans. At least you can say a few words."

"Yes," agreed the toy duck. "If

you squeeze me very hard, I sometimes squeak, but even that doesn't work if I've been left in the bath for a long time."

But Bernard just wasn't satisfied. "It's all very well," he said, "being content with what I can do already, but I'm an ambitious bear. I want to impress everyone I meet. I want people to say, 'Oh, yes, we know Bernard Bear. Isn't he amazing?' That's what I want."

"You should be careful, Bernard," said the toy train. "You might make matters worse, not better, with all your practising."

Nothing anyone could say would dissuade Bernard from

pursuing his singing career. He listened hard when the children in the nursery had their singsong each afternoon. He had soon learned the words and the tunes — but he still couldn't sing the songs! So Bernard listened even harder to what the teacher had to say.

"Now children," she said. "Lift up your heads and take deep breaths. I'm going to open the window so that you can breathe in all that lovely fresh air. Then we'll sing this song as loudly as we can. Let's see if we can't wake up Bernard Bear over there and make him growl!"

"I'm not asleep, actually,"

muttered Bernard, but it was nice to be mentioned, all the same.

When the children had gone home that night, Bernard thought about what the teacher had said. Fresh air! That was the answer. He must fill himself up with more fresh air.

Bernard hopped over to the window and nudged it open with his paw. It slid up quite easily.

"Now, the way to get most fresh air will be to sit on the windowsill," said Bernard to himself. "Let's see. If I put one leg this side and the other leg this side, I can *just* balance."

Bernard Bear sat on the

windowsill and took a deep breath.
Then he took another deep breath.
Then he took a third deep breath …
it was a breath too many. With a
wobble and a wiggle, Bernard Bear
overbalanced and fell right out of
the window.

Plop! Bernard fell heavily on to a flowerbed below the window. His face was muddy. His paws were muddy. His tummy was muddy. You would hardly have recognised him as the fine bear who sat on the nursery shelf.

Next day was sunny, so the teacher took the children outside. It wasn't very long before one little boy found Bernard in the flower-bed.

The teacher took charge at once. "Let me have a look at that bear," she said. "Oh dear, he's been outside all night, I think. I'll have to take him home with me and clean him up."

That night, the teacher did her best with Bernard Bear. She rubbed him and she scrubbed him, until his fur was as clean as ever. Then she brushed him with a lovely soft brush and put him near the radiator to dry.

"Phew!" said Bernard to himself. He felt that he had had a lucky escape.

Next day, looking as bright and bonny as usual, Bernard was taken back to the nursery. Two little girls immediately claimed him to join in their game.

"What do you say today, Bernard?" they asked, shaking him gently.

Bernard said nothing.

"Don't you want to talk to us, Bernard?" asked the little girls, poking the bear's tummy.

Bernard said nothing.

"Tell us who you are!" laughed the little girls, patting Bernard on the back.

But Bernard said not a word.

Whether it was the rubbing and the scrubbing, on the bump into the flowerbed, or simply being outside one whole night, there was no doubt about it. Bernard had lost his voice.

"If only I hadn't tried to sing," moaned Bernard to himself. "I had a lovely voice before, but now I'm just as silent as most other teddy bears.

I should have been happy with who I was."

Bernard certainly had learnt his lesson, and a few days later, when one of the children gave him a little shake, he found himself making a tiny noise.

"Grrrrr," he said. "Grrrr. Grrrr."

Perhaps Bernard will get his voice back after all. I hope so, don't you?

The Beep Beep Car

ONCE UPON A TIME, there was a teddy bear who had a car. Yes, he had a real car, in which he zoomed about all over the place. He visited his friends and took them for outings. He did shopping for toys who were too old or busy to go into town themselves. He even delivered cards and presents when it was Christmas time.

In fact, he was a very useful bear to know, and everything would have been fine if only he hadn't been so noisy. Well, it wasn't really the bear who was noisy. It was the car. Beep! Beep! Beep! Beep! It was terribly loud.

The teddy bear's friends never

had to look out of their windows to
see if he was coming. Oh no. From
miles away you could hear his car
beeping. There was plenty of time to
have a cup of tea, and read the
newspaper, and put your coat and
hat on before he arrived at your
door!

Some of the teddy's friends
tried to tackle him on the rather
tricky subject.

"Your car is a wonderful
machine," began the ragdoll, working
her way towards the important part.
"But tell me, does it have to make
such a loud beeping noise?"

"Oh yes," said the teddy bear.
"That's half the fun. Why, no one

would know I was coming if it wasn't for that beeping noise."

"That's very true," agreed the ragdoll, "but you know, there are times when we don't really want to know you are coming. I mean, the other week, for example, the poor old train jumped right off his tracks because you beeped as he was going round a corner. He did terrible damage to his axles, and he has only

started to get over the shock just recently."

"Well, I'm sorry to hear that," said the teddy bear, "but really that train is going to have to pull himself together. Whoever heard of a car that didn't go beep! beep! sometimes? I certainly never did."

"It's not so much that it goes beep! beep!" the doll went on. "It's that it does it so loudly."

"Well, you know," replied the teddy bear, "there's not much point in a beeper you can't hear. That's what they're for, you see."

The doll couldn't think of anything else to say after that. The teddy bear had a point in a way, but she still felt that his car was much, much louder than any other car she had ever heard (and that included the racing cars in their shiny box, and everyone knows what a loud noise they make!)

One day, the teddy bear decided to take some of his friends to the seaside. They packed up some sandwiches and their swimming costumes and set off along the road to the coast.

When they reached the seaside, the teddy bear parked his car as near to the sea as he could. Further along the beach, a policeman doll waved his arms at the toys.

"You see how everyone likes my car?" said the proud teddy.

The toys went down on to the beach and were soon having so much fun that not one of them noticed a little row of waves splashing on either side of them.

After some games and some sandwiches, the toys all had a snooze in the sunshine.

It was the ragdoll who woke up first, and she looked happily around.

"How lovely it is to be sitting on a little island like this," she said to herself. "Wait a minute … an island? This wasn't an island when we arrived!"

The waves were lapping on every side of the toys and the little

car. Anxiously, the ragdoll woke the other toys.

"It's too deep to wade," said the teddy bear. "How are we ever going to let anyone know that we are here? There's no one in sight at all. We could drown before help comes!"

But the ragdoll smiled. "I think your car's very loud beep is about to be useful," she said.

In two minutes, the toys were all inside the car, beeping the horn for all they were worth. At least, the teddy bear beeped, and the other toys kept their hands or their paws over their ears. Beep! Beep!

It was not long before the toys

were rescued by the waving policeman in a boat. "I did try to warn you," he said.

"What about my car?" asked the teddy bear, as they were rowed away. "I do hope the waves won't dampen its beep."

"We should be so lucky!" laughed the toys under their breath, now that they were safe and sound.

The Smiling Star

EVERY NIGHT, when Jenny was tucked up in bed, her mother said the same thing:

"Sweet dreams, darling. Shall we sing our bedtime song?"

And Jenny and her mummy would sing, ever so softly:

Star light, star bright,
First star I see tonight,
I wish I may, I wish I might,
Have the wish I wish tonight.

Then Jenny's mother would give her a kiss and put out the light. With the words of the song still ringing in her head, Jenny would crawl down to the foot of her bed

and peep through the curtains.
Sometimes it was cloudy, and there
were no stars to be seen. In the
summertime, it was often too light to
see the stars. But when she looked

out and saw a dark, clear sky, with little twinkling lights so high up and so far away, Jenny breathed a sigh of happiness. Then she shut her eyes and wished for the thing she wanted more than anything else in the world.

When she was a very tiny girl, Jenny wished for toys, or a visit to the playground, or even something really nice to eat for her supper next day. Sometimes her wishes came true, and sometimes they didn't, but

that wasn't really important because they were only little wishes. Now Jenny had a really big wish, and it mattered very much indeed whether it came true or not.

It had all started a few months before. Jenny's mummy and daddy started to have really big arguments. Jenny sometimes found her mummy in tears, although she brushed them quickly away when she saw her little girl. Daddy seemed unhappy too. He hugged Jenny and played with her as much as ever, but at breakfast and supper time, both he and Mummy were unusually quiet, with their eyes on their plates.

Jenny knew that something

was badly wrong, and at first she thought it was somehow her fault. She tried to be extra good and helpful. She tried not to talk more than she had to, and she just crept away when the horrid arguments started.

But one day, Jenny's mummy noticed how quiet and good she was being, and asked her what was the matter! Jenny explained that she was trying to make everything all right again, so that they could be a happy family.

Jenny's mummy hugged the little girl and sat her on her lap. She explained very gently that sometimes mummies and daddies don't get along so very well together. She reassured Jenny that it wasn't her fault in any way at all, and she promised that Jenny would not hear any more arguments.

After that, things were a little better. Jenny's mummy and daddy didn't argue in front of her, but Jenny was pretty sure that they still did it in private, because both of them had sad faces and were very quiet when they were together.

Then, one day, Jenny's daddy took her to the park to feed the ducks. As he and Jenny sat together on a bench, he explained that there were going to be some changes.

"I'm going to live in another

house in future," he said. "And you and Mummy will move to a little house somewhere very nice. I'll see you ever so often, and we'll have lots of fun together. I love you lots and lots and lots. Everything will be fine."

But Jenny couldn't help bursting into tears.

"I don't want you to go," she sobbed. "Please stay with us."

Jenny's daddy held her close and stroked her hair.

"I have to go, honey," he said. "Mummy and I both think it's the right thing to do, and in the end, we'll all be much happier. You and Mummy will have lovely times together, and when I come to see you, *we'll* have lovely times, too."

Jenny was still very upset, but she tried to be brave. Next day, Daddy didn't come home from work at his usual time.

"Daddy has gone to live in his new house," said Mummy. "And I have found us a lovely little cottage in the countryside. I know that you will like it, Jenny. There are cows and sheep and horses in the fields all around. And you will be able to have a rabbit of your own, if you like, just as you have always wanted."

That night, Jenny and her mummy sang their special song as usual:

Star light, star bright,
First star I see tonight,
I wish I may, I wish I might,
Have the wish I wish tonight.

For the first time, after her mother had closed the door, Jenny scuttled down to the end of the bed and peered at the sky as if her life depended on it. Thank goodness! There was one little star, twinkling in the sky.

"I wish my daddy would come home again," whispered Jenny, squeezing her eyes shut. "I wish it with all my heart."

All that week, Jenny made the same wish. Then, on Saturday, some men came with a truck and loaded all the furniture from the house into it.

"Come on, darling," said Jenny's mummy. "We're going to move into our new house today. I know that you will love it. Have you got all your toys?"

Jenny clutched her favourite teddy bear and followed mummy to the car. She looked back at the house where she had been so

happy, and tears rolled down her little cheeks.

"It will be all right, honey," said her mummy, hugging her. "I promise it will. New things are often upsetting, but everything will be fine."

"Everyone keeps saying that," sobbed Jenny, "but it isn't fine. It isn't all right."

Mummy started the car and looked as if she might cry too.

"It will be," she said. "Much sooner than you think, it will be."

On the way to the new house, Jenny and Mummy stopped for a snack at a little restaurant. Jenny knew that this was a special treat, and usually she would have loved it. But today the ice cream tasted horrible, and she couldn't finish her milkshake.

"I don't feel very well," she said, pushing her food away.

Mummy felt her forehead and looked at her carefully.

"Then we must hurry up to reach our new home," she said. "You can settle down and rest until you feel better. It's not much farther, and there's a surprise waiting for you there."

The countryside certainly was pretty, as they drove along the winding road to the little village where their new house was to be found. Even Jenny could not help noticing the pretty little lambs jumping in one field. There was nothing like that in the suburbs where she had lived before.

At last Mummy stopped the car and pointed to a little pink cottage with a thatched roof.

"That's where we're going to live," she said. "Isn't it nice?"

Jenny had to agree that the cottage did look pretty. It was the kind of place she had always wanted to live, only she had wanted to live there with her mummy *and* her daddy.

Mummy showed Jenny all over the cottage, including the little bedroom under the eaves that the little girl would have for her very own. Jenny peered out of the window and noticed that there would be a very good view of the stars in the night sky. So *that* would be all right.

"I'm not going to stop wishing just because we've moved here," she said to herself.

"Now," said Mummy, "come outside, and I'll show you your special surprise. Shut your eyes and take my hand."

Jenny followed her mother out into the garden. She felt the sun on her face and could smell lovely scents from the flowers as she passed them.

"Now," said Mummy, "open your eyes!"

Jenny opened them and blinked in the bright sunshine. Then she looked down at a little piece of grass with a fence around it.

"Oh!" cried Jenny. "Is he really for me?"

"Yes," smiled Mummy, for the

first time that day. "He's all yours.
What are you going to call him,
darling?"

Jenny looked at the dear little
white rabbit sitting on the grass.

"I'm going to call him
Snuffles," she said, "because of the
way he's wiggling his nose. Oh, he's
just what I always wanted. Look at
his lovely ears and his little pink
nose! I'm going to take ever such
good care of him."

"I know you will, sweetheart,"
said Mummy. "I've bought you a little
book about how to do it."

"Yes," said Jenny. "I want him to
stay with me always. I don't want
him to go away."

Jenny's mummy said nothing, as she went back into the cottage to start unpacking.

That night, Jenny slept for the first time in her new bedroom. She had her old bed, of course, and all her familiar things about her, but still it felt strange.

Mummy came in as usual to say goodnight and sing the Starlight Song. Jenny could hardly wait for her to close the door. Creeping out of her bed, she went over to the little window and looked out.

How much bigger and nearer the stars seemed than in the town, where the streetlights were so bright! Jenny gasped as she looked

up at the velvety night sky. There
was the moon, and there were
hundreds and hundreds of little stars
twinkling in the darkness.

Jenny looked at one star in
particular and made her wish. I'm
sure you can easily guess what it
was. The star seemed to twinkle as if
it was answering her.

Then Jenny crept back into her
bed and closed her eyes. It had been
a long, tiring day after all.

Almost at once, the little girl heard a tapping on the window. *Tap tap! Tap tap!* it went. Jenny didn't feel at all frightened. She just wondered very much what the strange sound was.

There was nothing else to do. The little girl got out of her bed once more and went to the window. There had not yet been time to put up new curtains, so she could see at once what was making the tapping sound, and she couldn't have been more surprised if Father Christmas himself had been sitting on the windowsill outside.

It was a star! Yes, a shiny yellow star with little arms and legs and a big beaming smile. Jenny rubbed her eyes. She knew that stars didn't come knocking on people's windows in the middle of the night.

But the little star knocked again. *Tap tap! Tap tap!* Almost without thinking, Jenny lifted the catch and opened the window.

"Good evening," said the star. "You wished?"

"Sorry?" said Jenny.

"*I'm* sorry," said the star. "Didn't that make sense? You wished, so I came. How can I help you this fine starry night?"

"I'm afraid I don't understand," said Jenny. "I've wished lots and lots of times, but I've never seen a star before."

"It's the interference," said the star. "It's a terrible problem for us. In towns there is so much light that children's messages often don't get through. But your wish was beautifully clear tonight. You'd like your daddy to come home, I believe. Now, you will get cold if you keep the

window open like this. I'll just hop inside and then we can talk properly. How would that be?"

Jenny was all too happy to invite the star into her bedroom. She hopped back into bed, and the star sat comfortably on the bedside table with his legs crossed. He was still smiling.

"Now," he said, "what has happened to your daddy?"

Then Jenny explained all about the arguments and the new houses. She even told the star about Snuffles.

"I see," said the star. "Poor you. Will you be able to see your daddy sometimes? Or has he gone to live a long way away?"

"Oh no," said Jenny. "He's very near, and he's coming to see me every weekend."

"Well, that is very good," said the star. "Now this kind of thing happens quite a lot, you know, and the best thing to do is always to wait a little while and see how things go. What I would like you to do is to spend a few weeks getting used to your new home. You can have fun with your daddy and with your mummy, and I will come to see you every night to make sure you are all right. Then we will have another little talk and see how things are going."

The star did sound as if he

knew what he was talking about, so Jenny agreed to do just what he suggested.

The next few weeks passed more quickly than she could have imagined. She met lots of new friends at her playgroup, and she explored the garden and the countryside beyond. There was a nice man who kept bees in the next cottage, and he had a little girl too, so Jenny and her new neighbour often played together.

At the weekends, Daddy came to see Jenny. They had lots of fun and talked about all kinds of things. In fact, they seemed to have a nicer time than they ever had before.

Daddy had so often been busy with work from the office or doing jobs around the house at the weekends.

Mummy seemed to be enjoying putting the new house in order too. She made pretty curtains for the windows and a beautiful rabbit hutch for Snuffles, who was as cosy as could be with his straw and his food and water.

All this time, Jenny carried on making the same wish each night. She didn't even have to think about it any more. The words came into her mind as soon as she looked out of her window and saw the stars.

"I wish my daddy could come and live with us," she said.

Each night, the smiling star came to visit Jenny. Sometimes he didn't stay very long, but at other times they sat and talked long into the night. When they had finished, Jenny would open the window, and the little star would whizz right up into the night sky.

The star talked about all kinds of things. He told Jenny about the North Pole and how cold it was there. He explained that it was cold like that in space, too, but that stars didn't mind. He described the many countries that he had seen on his travels and talked about the planets as if they were old friends. He told Jenny about some of the other children he visited, too.

Then one night, he said, "It's time we talked about your first wish, Jenny. I have some questions to ask you."

"All right," said the little girl. "What are they?"

"Would you say that your

mummy is happier now?" asked the smiling star.

Jenny thought about hearing her mummy singing as she made Snuffles' rabbit hutch. She remembered the fun they had had together, choosing new things for the house and deciding what to do in the big, rambling garden.

"Yes," she said. "I think she is much happier now."

"And is your daddy happier?" asked the smiling star.

Jenny thought about the way that daddy didn't have those creases in his forehead any more. She thought about all the lovely times she had had with him each weekend. He looked sort of younger somehow.

"Yes," said the little girl. "I think he *is* happier."

"And now for the really important question," said the star. "Are *you* happier, Jenny?"

Jenny thought hard. There were no more arguments. At mealtimes now, she chattered merrily. There were no more awkward silences. And it was lovely living in the country. And then there was Snuffles. She felt so grown up looking after him all by herself.

"Yes," she said. "I do feel happier too."

The smiling star smiled even

more broadly. "Then do you think
you should make a different wish
each night?" he asked. "Why don't
you think about it?" Jenny was rather
quiet the next day.

"Are you all right, darling?"
asked her mother.

"Yes, I am all right," said Jenny,
almost as if she was surprised to find
that she was. "We're both all right,
aren't we?"

"Yes, we are," smiled Mummy,
giving her a hug.

That weekend Jenny asked
Daddy if he was all right.

"I'm very all right," laughed
Daddy. "Race you to the swings!"

When Mummy came to say

goodnight that evening, she sang the special song with Jenny.

Star light, star bright,
First star I see tonight,
I wish I may, I wish I might,
Have the wish I wish tonight.

And Jenny looked out of the window and made a new wish.

"I wish we can all be happy, wherever we live," she said. And you know, her wish came true.

Mr Potter's Problem

IT WAS TWO O'CLOCK in the morning. As usual, Mr Potter was down in the kitchen, making himself a cup of tea. At two o'clock in the morning? Well, yes. You see Mr Potter simply couldn't sleep. Rather than lying awake, staring into the darkness, he felt it was better to come down and have a comforting cup of tea. At least from here he couldn't hear the dreadful noise.

You see, after thirty years of married life, Mr Potter's wife had started to snore. It wasn't just a gentle snuffling noise. It was an awful, trumpeting, elephant-on-the-warpath sort of noise. It was the kind of thing you couldn't sleep

through no matter how hard you
tried. And Mr Potter had tried very
hard indeed.

The first thing he had tried was
Mind over Matter. If I just pretend I
can't hear it, he thought, I *won't*
hear it, and I'll be able to get back
to sleep.

Well, I don't know if you've
ever *tried* to sleep through a
deafening elephant-on-the-warpath
trumpeting noise, but it's not very
easy. Just as the echo of the snore is
dying away, and you are drifting off
to sleep again, an ear-splitting blast
hits you amidships.

Mr Potter was a practical man,
so the next thing he tried was

Double Strength Ear Plugs. The label on the packet claimed that you could sleep through a hurricane

with this wonderful product in place. Well, maybe you could, but you couldn't sleep through Mrs Potter's snoring, as Mr Potter can confirm. It was slightly softer, oh yes, and sort of muffled too, but in a way that was worse. With ear plugs in, Mr Potter felt as though the noise was inside his own head. It was really horrible.

Now you will be asking, why didn't Mr Potter do the sensible thing and hop off to spend the night in the spare room, where the snoring would sound like a faraway bugle call. Well, Mr Potter was a really kind man, and he was determined that his wife wouldn't find out about her problem from *him*. You see, Mrs Potter was a proud and proper woman. She wouldn't have dreamed of letting the next-door neighbours see her in her curlers or of wearing her slippers in the street. Her kind husband knew that she would be mortified if she knew about the snoring, so he was doing everything he could to keep the news from her, but, oh dear, the poor man was beginning to feel faint from lack of sleep!

Mr Potter went to the library to read up about the causes of snoring. Before long he had a whole pile of books open in front of him. It seemed that there were as many views about how to solve the problem as there were people who snored.

But one paragraph caught Mr Potter's eye. It claimed that a lack of fresh air could make matters worse.

That night, as they were getting ready for bed, Mr Potter said casually to his wife, "It's quite warm tonight, my dear. Do you mind if we have the window open a little? I read in the paper that it's terribly important to have plenty of fresh air when you get to our age."

"It's terribly important not to catch pneumonia too," said his wife, "but I suppose it *isn't* very cold tonight, so if you'd like the window open, that's fine."

Mr Potter smiled to himself as he opened the window wide. Maybe this would do the trick.

Fifteen minutes later, Mr Potter was off to make an early cup of tea. The noise seemed *worse*! He was so tired that he actually nodded off at the kitchen table … and woke up five hours later with a stiff neck, just in time to crawl back to bed for another couple of hours of elephants.

Next morning, Mr Potter took himself off to the park for a brisk walk to clear his head. While he was gone, there came a knock at the door. When Mrs Potter went to answer it, she found her next-door neighbour looking embarrassed on the doorstep.

"Excuse me, Mrs Potter," said Mrs Maybury. "I wonder if I could have a word? It's a rather delicate matter, so perhaps I could come inside?"

"By all means," said Mrs Potter, who certainly didn't want the world and his wife knowing her business.

When the two ladies were sitting comfortably in the living room, Mrs Maybury seemed to be having some difficulty in knowing where to begin.

"Are you feeling quite well?" asked Mrs Potter. "You look pale."

"The fact is," said Mrs Maybury, grateful for a place to start, "I haven't had a wink of sleep all night. That's why I've come."

Mrs Potter was puzzled. "I'm not sure how I can help," she said slowly.

"You see, the reason I can't sleep," confessed Mrs Maybury, "is your husband."

Mrs Potter almost fell out of her chair. For one wild moment she imagined that Mrs Maybury had taken a fancy to Mr Potter and was unable to sleep for thinking of him. Then she pulled herself together and realised she was being ridiculous.

Mr Potter was a dear, sweet man, and the love of her life, but he was hardly the stuff that dreams are made of.

"I shall have to ask you to explain," said Mrs Potter rather stiffly to her neighbour.

"Oh, please don't be angry," cried Mrs Maybury, hearing Mrs Potter's tone. "I know it's embarrassing, but we have lived next door to each other for twelve years now. We should be able to talk about these things like mature human beings."

"But what things?" asked Mrs

Potter, feeling as though she was
wading through treacle.

"Why, Mr Potter's *snoring*," said
Mrs Maybury.

Mrs Potter was more surprised
than she would have been if Mrs
Maybury *had* conceived a passion
for Mr Potter.

"His snoring?" she gasped.

"Yes," moaned Mrs Maybury. "We
hear it every night, you know. The
walls are quite thick between our
houses. I never hear your television
or your vacuum cleaner or anything.
But that snoring positively shakes
the walls! We've been hearing it for
some time, but it wasn't loud
enough to disturb us, and I didn't

like to say anything. Last night was the final straw. I think you had your window open, and we did too. It was deafening! I lay awake all night, and so did my husband."

"Indeed?" said Mrs Potter coldly. She didn't take kindly to criticism, and Mrs Maybury was beginning to annoy her. "I can truthfully say that it has never disturbed *me*," she went on, "but then I am a sound sleeper, not *foolishly nervous* or worried by *silly little things*. I do realise that not everyone has my excellent health and clear conscience."

"Well, I did feel I should mention it," said Mrs Maybury, rising to her feet.

"And I'm very glad you did so,"
said Mrs Potter warmly. "I do hope
it has helped you to get it off your
chest, my dear."

Mrs Potter showed her
neighbour to the door, and Mrs
Maybury, feeling oddly as though it
was *she* who had the problem,
hurried home to report to her
husband that the meeting had not
been an unqualified success.

As soon as she had closed the
front door, Mrs Potter picked up
the telephone and got to work. She
knew perfectly well that her
neighbour was a truthful woman,
and she didn't doubt for a moment
that what she had said was true,

although it certainly was extraordinary that she herself had never been woken by Mr Potter's snoring. Mrs Potter was taking no chances. She didn't want any more neighbours coming round to complain, and she wasn't going to run the risk of her own sleep being disturbed, now that she knew about Mr Potter's "Little Problem".

By the time her husband came home from his walk, Mrs Potter had made her plans and was ready to put them into action. She made Mr Potter a cup of tea and asked him to sit down as she had something serious to say.

"Now, Alfred," she said, "you

know that I've never been one to beat about the bush. I like to call a spade a spade. The fact is that the neighbours have been complaining about your snoring, so I've had to *take steps*. I've ordered a double-glazing firm to start work tomorrow, and, as I really can't afford to lose my sleep, I wondered if you could stay in the spare room until your little problem is better. I do realise you can't help it, dear."

Mr Potter opened his mouth to protest. Then he realised that his problems were at an end.

"Of course, dear," he said.